D060443

AUNT ZINNIA
and the Ogre

For a free color catalog describing Gareth Stevens' list of
high-quality books, call 1-800-341-3569 (USA)
or 1-800-461-9120 (Canada).

Beechwood Bunny Tales
Dandelion's Vanishing Vegetable Garden
Mistletoe and the Baobab Tree
Periwinkle at the Full Moon Ball
Poppy's Dance
Aunt Zinnia and the Ogre
Violette's Daring Adventure
Family Moving Day

Library of Congress Cataloging-in-Publication Data

Huriet, Geneviève.
    [Tante Zinia et l'ogre Kazoar. English]
    Aunt Zinnia and the ogre / written by Geneviève Huriet;
illustrated by Loïc Jouannigot.
        p. cm. — (Beechwood bunny tales)
    Summary: Aunt Zinnia tells her bunny nieces and nephews
a cautionary tale about a skirmish with a noisy ogre that shone
a bright light, one dark night when she defied her parents'
admonishment to stay away from the highway.
    ISBN 0-8368-0910-6
    [1. Rabbits—Fiction. 2. Obedience—Fiction. 3. Aunts—
Fiction. 4. Motorcycles—Fiction.] I. Jouannigot, Loïc, ill.
II. Title. III. Series. IV. Series: Huriet, Geneviève.
Beechwood bunny tales.
PZ7.H95657Au 1992   [E]—dc20   92-32875

North American edition first published in 1992 by
Gareth Stevens Publishing
1555 North RiverCenter Drive, Suite 201
Milwaukee, Wisconsin 53212, USA

11/23/98

English text by Amy Bauman

Printed in the United States of America

 2 3 4 5 6 7 8 9 97

BEECHWOOD BUNNY TALES

AUNT ZINNIA
and the Ogre

written by GENEVIÈVE HURIET
illustrated by LOÏC JOUANNIGOT

Gareth Stevens Publishing
MILWAUKEE

It was a beautiful autumn evening in Beechwood Grove, and the Bellflower family had just finished a delicious dinner of carrots, salad, and sugared apples. Aunt Zinnia got up to clear the table. Papa Bramble and his five little bunnies joined her. With seven of them working, the kitchen was clean in no time. Little by little, everyone gathered in the living room, where Bramble started a cheery fire in the fireplace.

"Papa, will you tell us a story?" Violette asked when everyone had gathered.

"I'll tell the bunnies a story about Kazoar the Ogre," said Aunt Zinnia, " — a true story!"

The bunnies gathered around Aunt Zinnia.

"Many years ago, there was a clever little bunny. She ran fast, danced well, and knew how to bake the most delicious cakes. But she was stubborn and wasn't afraid of anything."

"What was her name?" Violette asked.

"We'll call her Zinnia," said Aunt Zinnia.

"One day, Zinnia was invited to help pick apples at her friend Cleo's home. Apple-picking days were more fun than work, and Cleo's family always had a wonderful picnic when the work was done.

" 'Zinnia,' her mother said to her that day, 'Now listen closely. Our neighbors, the Meadows, will bring you home. It will be dark then, so you must stay with them. And remember, stay away from the highway, okay?'

" 'I know, Mama, I hear what you say. The highway, the highway is no place to play,' Zinnia sang. She laughed, kissed her mother, and ran off to join her friends.

"What a day! The trees were bent nearly in half under the weight of the apples, and the picnic was magnificent. When everyone finished eating, they sang, and the grandmothers told stories of ogres and fairies.

"But as soon as the moon rose, the Meadows wanted to leave. Reluctantly, Zinnia went with them.

"'Goodnight, Zinnia! Watch out for Kazoar the Ogre on your way home!' her friends called to her.

"'He doesn't scare me!' she laughed.

"It wasn't long before Zinnia wished she had gone home with anyone but the Meadows. They were afraid of everything: people, dogs, foxes, wolves. The slightest noise sent them running for the underbrush, crying:

'Listen! Did you hear that noise?'
'Hide, everyone! Lower your heads!'

"Zinnia quickly had enough running and hiding. She began
watching for a chance to slip away. The next time the group ran for
the bushes, she darted from the path and toward the highway.

"No one saw her stray.

"'If I take the highway, I'll get to the village before them,' Zinnia
thought. 'Won't they be surprised to find me waiting for them!'

"That night, the highway was dark and deserted. Zinnia was no longer sure that her plan was such a good one. All of a sudden, Zinnia heard a strange, grinding sound behind her: 'Zuuin, zuuin!'

"She began to run. As the noise grew louder, she turned and saw a strange light. It glowed brighter and brighter until it caught up with Zinnia. Then, in front of her, rose the long, black shadow of — Kazoar the Ogre!

"By now, Zinnia was nearly out of breath. She jumped to the left. The ogre overtook her. She jumped to the right. His hoarse laughter followed her: 'Drin, rinn, rinn.'

"Finally, with one last burst of strength, she threw herself in the ditch. The light ran on past her, and after a while, she could no longer hear the noise. The ogre had lost her trail!"

In the Bellflower living room, the five little bunnies gasped.

"Was Kazoar the Ogre gone for good?" asked Dandelion in a very little voice. He leaned against Violette.

Aunt Zinnia held up a finger and went on. "For a few moments, Zinnia lay at the bottom of the ditch, trembling and barely daring to breathe. Her paws and little nose were so cold.

"'I have to find the Meadows,' she said to herself. She picked herself up out of the ditch and scurried back onto the highway. Everything was deserted again.

"Her heart beating, Zinnia began walking again. Finally, in the distance, she saw the path the Meadows had taken. She was sure she could find them, and she began to run.

"But suddenly, over the hill came the ogre again. This time, he seemed much larger. His gleam shone stronger, and he was making a much more frightening noise. 'Braoum, broum, broum. Braoum, broum, broum,' he roared.

"Zinnia knew the ogre was furious now. As his voice echoed in the silence of the night, his shadow shot up in front of her. Panic-stricken, Zinnia zigzagged back and forth, hoping to escape him once again. But he caught up with her and knocked her roughly aside. The force sent Zinnia spinning across the road!"

The little bunnies listened to the story, their eyes wide. How was little Zinnia going to get herself out of this?

"Once again," their aunt went on, "the ogre disappeared. Zinnia crawled under a thorny bush to hide. By now, she knew the Meadows would be looking for her. But they would be looking along the pathway, she realized sadly. They wouldn't search the highway, where she had promised never to go!

"Just then, it began to rain. Tired and now wet, Zinnia squatted in the mud, unable to budge without hurting her shoulder. Suddenly, she saw two figures marching toward her in the ditch. In the darkness, she could not see who or what they were. Her heart began to beat with worry. Were these ogres again?

"The two strangers talked quietly to each other, examining the ditch as they walked.

"'I'm almost certain I heard something,' one said to the other. In the light of their lantern, Zinnia saw that the two strangers were rabbits.

"'Over here!' she whimpered as they turned to leave. 'Please help me.'

"'Poor bunny!' said the oldest one. 'You're hurt!'

"'Where do you live?' the other asked. 'We'll take you there. Lean on me.'"

"Aunt Zinnia, was that little bunny you?" Poppy interrupted.

Aunt Zinnia smiled and nodded. "Yes . . . a very long time ago, Poppy."

"Was your mama angry?" asked Mistletoe.

"My poor parents had such a scare, and I was in such bad shape that they were too busy nursing me to even think about being angry," she answered.

"Papa," said Violette, "did you know the two brave rabbits?"

"You all know them," said Bramble. "It was your grandfather Theo and his brother Leo who, much later, married Aunt Zinnia. Now, time for bed, little bunnies. Dandelion is almost asleep now."

The whole family climbed the stairs to the boys' room. Opening one eye, Dandelion mumbled, "Bad ogre . . ." and then fell back asleep.

"Kazoar the Ogre doesn't come to houses, does he?" Periwinkle asked nervously.

"You're safe here, little bunnies," said Bramble. "Kazoar the Ogre is only dangerous to bunnies who dawdle on the highway." He winked at Aunt Zinnia, and the bunnies fell asleep, feeling happy and safe.